dedicated to
Daniel Jeannette
who first told me about
the Sock Monster, & inspired
me to write about it.

KO KIDS BOOKS
www.kokidsbooks.com

Distributed by Publishers Group West
1.800.788.3123 / www.pgw.com

Publisher's Cataloging-in-Publication (Provided by Quality Books, Inc.): Otoshi, Kathryn
Simon and the sock monster / written & illustrated by Kathryn Otoshi. –1st ed.
p. cm. Summary: Simon loses his lucky soccer sock and thinks a Sock Monster ate it for dinner. ISBN 0-9723946-1-3
1. Socks – Juvenile fiction. 2. Monster– Juvenile fiction. [1. Socks – Fiction. 2. Monster– Fiction.] I. Title.
PZ7.O8777Si 2004 [E] QBI33-01798

Book Design by Kathryn Otoshi
Printed in Hong Kong

"Not again," groaned Simon, holding up one freshly cleaned sock. "Now where did my other one go?" This wasn't just any old sock. This was Simon's lucky soccer sock. His championship game was today, and he never played without it.

"Hey, Janey," called Simon to his older sister. "My lucky soccer sock's gone. Have you seen it?"

"Hmmm," said Janey thoughtfully. "Did you check under the bed?"

"I've checked in the bed, on it, AND under. I've checked everywhere! It's just vanished – without a trace!"

"Well then," said Janey. "It looks like the Sock Monster must have struck again!"

"Sock Monster!" cried Simon. "There's no Sock Monster!"

"Sure there is," said Janey. "Every home has one. When Sock Monsters get hungry, they slither around in people's basements looking for lost socks to eat. Where did you think all those missing socks go to? Sock Monsters have to eat too, you know!"

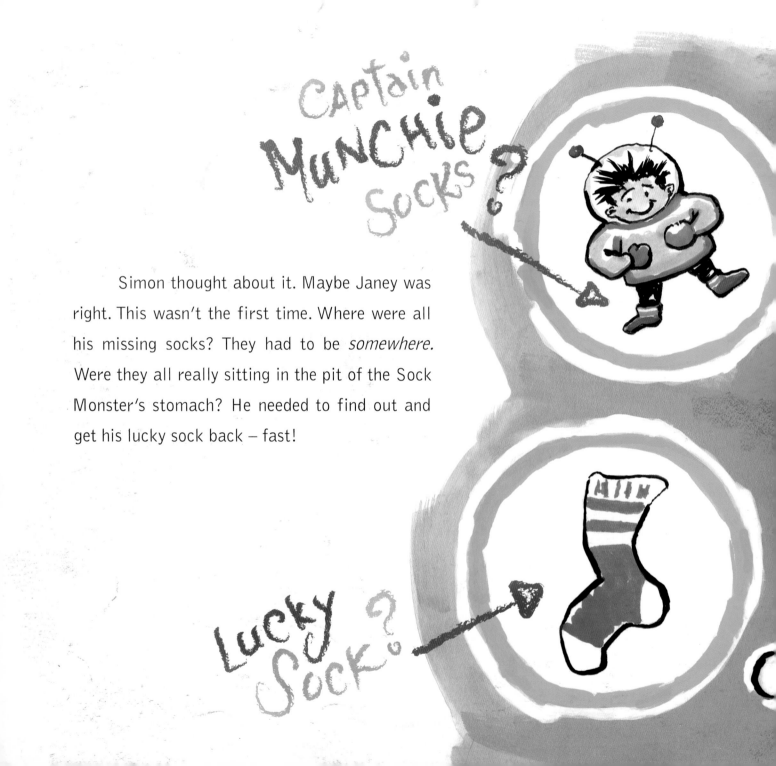

Captain **Munchie** Socks?

Lucky Sock?

Simon thought about it. Maybe Janey was right. This wasn't the first time. Where were all his missing socks? They had to be *somewhere*. Were they all really sitting in the pit of the Sock Monster's stomach? He needed to find out and get his lucky sock back – fast!

Simon ran next door to tell his best friend, Timmy. Maybe he'd just laugh and say it was all a joke. But Timmy didn't laugh. "I have an entire drawer filled with socks that don't match," he said, his eyes wide. "I wonder what a Sock Monster looks like? I mean, when's the last time anyone's seen one?"

"Or been left alive to report one!" gulped Simon. "They must stay out of sight by hiding under the washing machine – or even in it!"

"Then they pounce on the lost sock, shredding it to bits with their sharp teeth until nothing's left!" exclaimed Timmy.

"My poor lucky sock!" cried Simon.

"Can't you play without it?" asked Timmy.

"No way!" moaned Simon. "I've scored six goals with it on. I can't kick straight without it. If we don't find it, we might lose our big game. We have to rescue it!"

Simon put on his bike helmet and took his martian dart gun for protection, and Timmy used a frisbee as a shield.

They pushed open the basement door, and it swung open with a long, loud CREEEEEEEK!

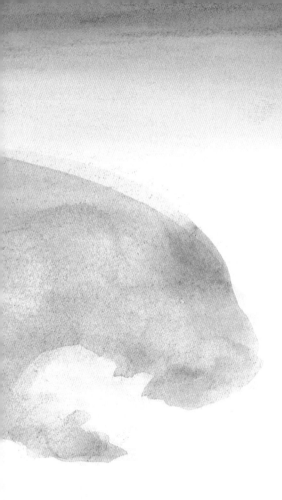

Simon took a step. Something green and sticky was oozing down the stairs. Ugh! Sock Monster slime! A strange noise sounded from the corner of the basement.

"Did you hear that?" hissed Timmy.

Down below, the lights started to flicker.

Simon and Timmy tiptoed down the stairs. Something soft squished beneath Simon's shoe. He bent down to pick it up. It was part of a sock, ripped to shreds. He grabbed Timmy's arm. Something big was coming their way. It was getting louder and LOUDER...closer and CLOSER! Simon couldn't look. His heart was beating a mile a minute!

Suddenly a HUGE shadow loomed and grew right before their eyes. It reared back its neck to attack!

AAAHHHHH!!!

Simon's dart gun arrow flew crazily up in the air, and Timmy ducked behind his frisbee. Timmy screamed, Simon screamed, and the Sock Monster screamed!

"SIMON! TIMMY! What are you doing down here? You two nearly scared me to death!" said his startled mom.

She was standing on a ladder, putting in a new light bulb.

"There's a Sock Monster in the basement," blurted Simon. "It has my lucky soccer sock and we need to rescue it before the Sock Monster eats it for dinner!"

"What? Did you say, 'Sock Monster'?" asked Simon's mom, picking up the detergent bottle. A tiny leak of slimy, green liquid oozed from the bottom of the bottle.

"Simon, have you really checked everywhere? Under the bed? In your closet? It's probably right under our noses. Let's go to your room. We'll find it," said Simon's mom.

Together they found a whole stack of socks that Simon thought he'd never see again. But still no lucky sock. Time was running out!

Just then Janey tapped on his door. "Hey, Simon," she said. "I heard you haven't found your sock yet. Listen, I meant to tell you earlier, but there's really no such thing as a –"

"Hey, look! My Captain Munchie socks!" said Simon, pulling them from underneath his dresser. He was happy to see them – even if they weren't *lucky*.

Found

Found

still missing

"Why don't you play with those?" said Janey. "You don't need special socks to win. Just play like you always do."

And then a new thought came to Simon: he had gone to the basement to face a Sock Monster, and he'd done it *without* his lucky sock! That was the bravest thing he'd ever done. Could he play this championship game without his lucky sock too?

Why not? He hopped around on one foot trying to put his Captain Munchie socks on, and tripped right over Buster. That dog was always in the way! Buster tried to yelp, but he had something in his mouth as usual.

And that's when it hit Simon.

trip over Buster

He grabbed Buster's face and pried open his slobbery mouth. AND THERE INSIDE WAS HIS LUCKY SOCK! It was chewed to bits with dog drool all over it. Simon wiped his shredded sock on his pants.

Good as new!...or not.

"Some Sock Monster," snorted Timmy as they all ran to the game.

the winning team

RIGHT into the Net

uh-oh!

Simon kicked the ball so hard for the winning goal, his shoe flew right off his foot! Buster ran over to grab his shoe with his big slobbery mouth. "Uh-oh," laughed Simon. "I hope I get my shoe back!"

Simon was so happy, he put on his shredded lucky sock for fun and gave his foot a kiss. Janey saw him do it and made a face. "EWWWWW!" she said. "The Germ Monsters will get you for that!"

Simon didn't care.

the end.